Terrible Tuesday

Story by Hazel Townson

Pictures by Tony Ross

Andersen Press · London
Hutchinson of Australia

For my granddaughter
VICTORIA JANE HINDLE
Born 9th August 1984
H.T.

For PHILIPPA
T.R.

British Library Cataloguing in Publication Data
Townson, Hazel
  Terrible Tuesday.
  I. Title   II. Ross, Tony
  823'.914[J]   PZ7
  ISBN 0-86264-098-9

Terry was pretending to be an aeroplane. As he zoomed through the hall, he heard his mum talking on the telephone.

"Tuesday will be TERRIBLE!" she said. "I'm dreading it! You just would not believe how scared I am!"

Terry zoomed out into the garden. There he crash-landed on the lawn and lay wondering why Tuesday was going to be so terrible.

Maybe all the shops would close on Tuesday? How nice to escape the boring queues!

But it would be terrible if there were no sweets or ice-cream —
only plain ordinary food.

Maybe robbers were going to come and steal all the furniture on Tuesday? Some of it was old and shabby anyway. Some of it took up too much room.

But it *would* be terrible to have no bed, no chairs and no umbrella-stand.

Maybe, thought Terry, someone is going to kidnap ME on Tuesday! He longed to have an adventure, with everyone chasing after him.

But it *would* be terrible for Mum and Dad to have to manage without him.

Maybe there was to be a flood on Tuesday? Terry thought water was fun, but he knew his mother could not swim.

She *would* think it terrible if her face went under water.

Maybe thieves were planning to rob Dad's bank on Tuesday?
Dad could foil them and be a hero. Fancy seeing your own
dad on television news!

But it *would* be terrible if the thieves tied Dad to a table-leg
and gagged him with a duster.

Maybe a witch was going to fly in through the window and set up house in the loft on Tuesday? Terry thought he would like to make friends with a witch and learn spells.

But it *would* be terrible if she turned the family into toads.

Maybe a wild tiger was going to escape from the zoo on Tuesday? Terry thought it was a pity to keep tigers in cages.

But it *would* be terrible to peep round a corner and find one peeping back.

Maybe a ghost, who had been asleep in the cellar for a hundred years, was going to wake up on Tuesday? Terry thought it would be fun to play with a ghost and help with a haunting.

But it *would* be terrible if his parents got so scared that they ran away.

Maybe Martians were going to land in the garden on Tuesday? It would be fun to see whether they looked like daleks or robots or wobbly blobs.

But it *would* be terrible if you suddenly found yourself halfway to the moon.

Maybe a whirlwind was due on Tuesday? A whirlwind must make a wonderful whoosh.

But it *would* be terrible to watch all your favourite things blown far away, for ever.

Maybe the sky was going to fall on Tuesday? Well, the sun, moon, stars and little white fluffy clouds would look good in the garden on stems and branches.

But it *would* be terrible to have a great Nothing overhead, like a huge, empty upside-down basin.

At last Terrible Tuesday came. Terry woke feeling excited. This was THE DAY! Today he would know what the terrible happening was going to be.

But all that happened was that his favourite cousins came to tea.